THE
READ-
TO-ME
TREASURY

SELECTED AND EDITED BY
SALLY GRINDLEY

ILLUSTRATED BY
TONI GOFFE

DOUBLEDAY
NEW YORK LONDON TORONTO SYDNEY AUCKLAND

PUBLISHED BY DOUBLEDAY
a division of Bantam Doubleday Dell Publishing Group, Inc.
666 Fifth Avenue, New York, New York 10103

DOUBLEDAY
and the portrayal of an anchor with a dolphin
are trademarks of Doubleday,
a division of Bantam Doubleday Dell Publishing Group, Inc.

For permission to reproduce copyright material, acknowledgment and thanks are due to the following: Victor Gollancz Ltd on the author's behalf for "Because of Figs" by Ann Cameron from *The Julian Stories;* Methuen Children's Books Ltd on the author's behalf for "Naughty Daisy" by Joyce Gillham from *The Read-Me-Another-Story Book* compiled and edited by Dorothy Edwards; Jonathan Cape Ltd on the author's behalf for "The Little Boy's Secret" by David L. Harrison from *The Book of Giant Stories* illustrated by Philippe Fix; and A D Peters & Co. Ltd on the author's behalf for "The Magpie's Nest" by Michael Rosen from *Story Chest* published by Viking Kestrel. The other stories appear for the first time in this collection. Permissions granted by the authors.

Library of Congress Cataloging-in-Publication Data
The Read-to-me treasury/selected by Sally Grindley: illustrated by Toni Goffe.—1st ed.
p.   cm.
Summary: A collection of fourteen stories by a variety of authors on such subjects as Indian elephants, giants, ghosts, measles, magpies, and Dad's old working boots.
1. Children's stories, English. 2. Children's stories, American.
[1. Short stories. 2. Humorous stories.] I. Grindley, Sally.
II. Goffe, Toni, ill.
PZ5.R19845 1990
[E]—dc20   89-35951   CIP   AC
ISBN 0-385-26677-4

CONTENTS

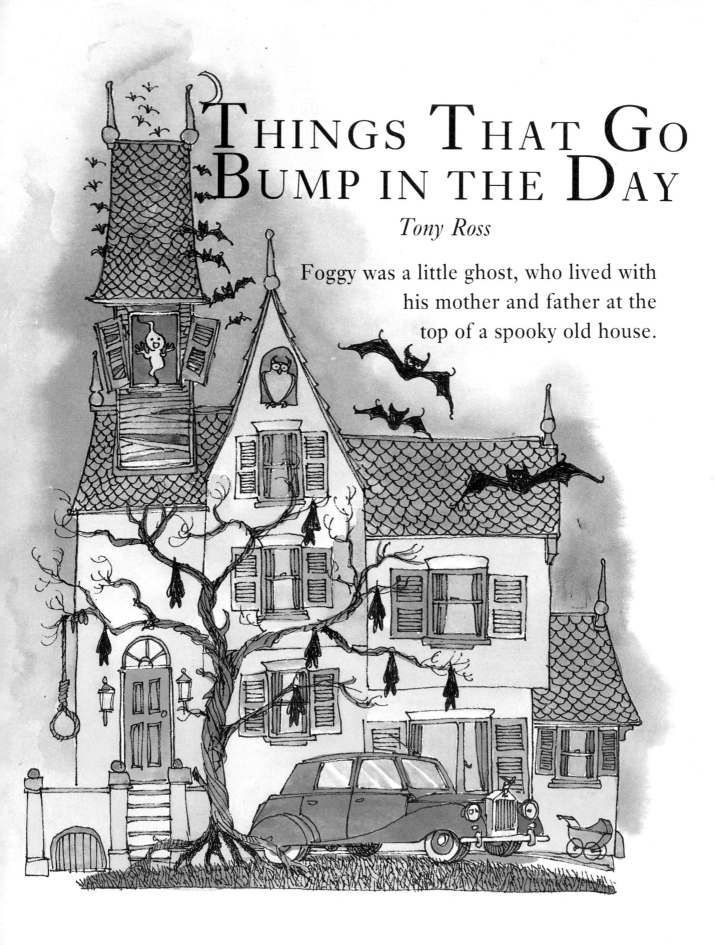

THINGS THAT GO BUMP IN THE DAY

Tony Ross

Foggy was a little ghost, who lived with
his mother and father at the
top of a spooky old house.

Foggy was born only about five hundred years ago, so he was a very young ghost. He had lived in lots of places, including a castle, but this was the best. Ghost families like spooky old places because they make them feel safe. This one had lots of bats and spiders for pets. There were wood licc too, but they make rotten pets. You can't teach them anything, and they are not very playful. Foggy nearly taught a wood louse to sit up and beg, but it kept falling on its back and kicking its legs in the air.

Foggy loved being a ghost. But sometimes life got a little BORING. There are not many things a ghost can do. Then Foggy found a book of ghost stories, and things began to get better. The first story was about a ghost who walked through walls. "That'll be a FABULOUS thing to do!" said Foggy to a creepy slug. And he walked BONK into a wall. All he did, though, was bump his nose.

"Shouldn't believe everything you read," giggled the creepy slug.

The next story was about a ghost who walked all over a house, shouting "OOOOOHHH!" and waving his hands in the air and jumping out of dark places. Foggy thought that was a silly way to behave, but he couldn't get the story out of his mind. There was a whole house beyond the dusty rooms where Foggy lived. Maybe wandering around that going "OOOOOHHH!" would be less boring than teaching wood lice to sit up and beg.

That morning, when it was time to go to sleep, Foggy's mom gave him a cobweb sandwich and a glass of slime. Then she tucked him into bed.

"Mom," said Foggy, "what's it like in the rest of the house? Are there any dark places?"

Mom kissed Foggy on the bump at the end of his nose.

"Don't you dare go into the rest of the house," she warned. "The rest of the house is a TERRIBLE place. Your dad went there once and said it was really scary. He said it was horribly CLEAN, and smelled of SOAP, with sunlight all over the place and lots of knobs on everything. UGH!" She shuddered.

Foggy curled up and pretended to go to sleep. The rest of the house sounded exciting, just like an adventure in a book.

When he was sure his mom and dad were asleep, Foggy got up. He went to the door and, making himself very small, he slithered through the keyhole into the rest of the house.

Foggy floated at the top of some stairs. It was true what Mom had said. The house was horribly light, with a funny smell. "That must be soap," shivered Foggy.

Slowly he went down the stairs. He hovered in the air a little, because there was tickly, furry stuff spread all over the floor. He looked around for a friendly bat, even a wood louse, but there weren't any. "Even the creepies daren't come into this awful place," he said to himself.

With bated breath, the little ghost floated along the

landing. His heart pounded inside him, and he was FAR too frightened to go "OOOOOHHH!" Foggy wasn't a particularly brave ghost, and by now he was getting really scared. The rest of the house wasn't a good place.

Foggy turned to go back the way he'd come. Then he saw it! If he'd had a skin, he'd have jumped right out of it. It was HORRIBLE.

It was very big, and it was lumbering along clutching a small model of itself. It had blue eyes, with hairs all around them, and matted yellow hair hung in twists down its back. Worst of all, when it opened its mouth to snarl, it showed fearsome white fangs. And it smelled of SOAP.

Foggy reeled. Back along the landing he fled, waving his arms in the air, and shouting "OOOOOOHHHH!" Up the stairs, through the keyhole, to where his mom and dad sat up in bed, wakened by all the commotion.

"Mom," shouted Foggy. "I'VE SEEN A LITTLE GIRL!"

"Don't be silly," said Mom, cuddling her son. "There's no such thing as little girls."

8

SAM PLAYS THE TRUMPET

Gabriel Alington

Every day Sam asked the same question.

"Are we going to the park today?"

The park was his favorite place, because right in the middle was a big round bandstand where each afternoon the Brass Band played. Sam sat on the grass in front of all the chairs and listened to the music. It was fine music, loud and exciting. The bandsmen and bandswomen wore red jackets and smart peaked caps. Some of them played trumpets, and their bright, shiny instruments gleamed in the sun. Sam's mother sat beside him with his small sister, Rosie, till Rosie got bored and had to be taken to see the ducks. Sam never got bored listening to the band. He was going to be a bandsman when he grew up.

"I'll play the trumpet," he said, "and I'll wear a red jacket like the people in the band."

On his fifth birthday his mother and father gave him a trumpet. It was bright and shiny like the trumpets in the band. Sam took a deep breath and blew into the end, but no sound came out. He tried again, puffing out his cheeks. Still nothing happened. Then his father had a turn. He blew and he blew and his face went very pink, but the trumpet would not make a single toot.

"It needs a lot of practice," Sam's father said. "You'll have to keep at it."

Sam did keep at it. He took the trumpet to the park and blew it all the time the band was playing. But no toot came out. Then one day, toward the end of the concert when the music rose to a mighty peak, there was a moment's pause. The conductor waited with both arms raised, the whole audience held their breath — except for Sam. He went on blowing. And suddenly, to his great surprise, the trumpet gave a TOOT, loud and shrill. TOOT, TOOT, TOOT, it went.

Everyone around him turned and stared.

"Shush," they all said. "Shush. Be quiet."

Sam blushed and stared at his shoes, but he could not help smiling. He had TOOTED his trumpet! He wished his mother would come back from the duck pond so that he could tell her.

When the concert was over, one of the trumpet players in the band beckoned to Sam.

"Me?" said Sam, pointing to his chest.

The Bandsman nodded and beckoned again, so Sam took his trumpet and climbed the steps onto the bandstand.

"That's a pretty nice instrument you've got there," the Bandsman said.

TOOT! TOOT! TOOT!

.Sam held out his trumpet. "You can blow it if you like."

"We'll swap," said the Bandsman, handing Sam his.

It was big and very heavy, and when Sam blew into it no noise came out. Then the Bandsman tried Sam's. Nothing happened. He tried again — and again.

"It's a bit difficult," Sam said.

"You show me then," said the Bandsman, giving the trumpet back to Sam. So Sam showed him. TOOT, TOOT, TOOT.

"That's splendid," said the Bandsman. "You'll be a fine trumpeter one day."

He turned and called the rest of the band. "Hey, come and hear this." The others gathered around Sam while he played for them. TOOT, TOOT, TOOT.

When Sam's mother and Rosie came back from the duck pond, they were surprised to see him on the bandstand. Sam waved to them and played an extra-loud TOOT. His mother laughed and clapped her hands. Rosie clapped too. And then all the bandsmen and bands women clapped as well. Sam blushed again and stared at his shoes.

He felt he would burst with happiness.

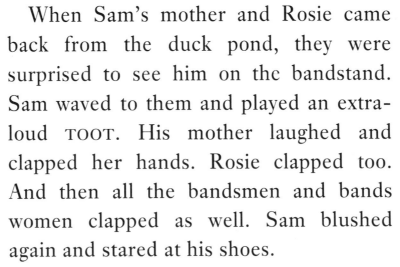

NAUGHTY DAISY

Joyce Gillham

There was once a cow and this cow's name was DAISY.

Daisy the cow lived in a field, with NINE other cows.

(MooO-OO-OO. MooO-OO-OO.)

Every afternoon, when the farmer came to take the cows home to bed, that naughty Daisy would run away and HIDE.

And her big, fat body would shake WITH LAUGHTER.

(Hoo-Hoo! Hoo-Hoo!)

NAUGHTY DAISY!

When the farmer called, "Daisy, where are you?" she would shake and shake with laughter.

NAUGHTY DAISY!

Day after day, when he collected the cows, he would count them as they went through the gate:

1, 2, 3, 4, 5, 6, 7, 8, 9!

Nine good cows, but oh dear! NO DAISY AGAIN.

So: first he looked behind a tree. *NO* DAISY.

Then he looked behind the water trough. *NO* DAISY.

Then he looked in the ditch. *NO* DAISY.

Then he looked under the privet hedges. NO DAISY.

Then at last he looked behind a bush.

"Hoo-oo. Hoo!"

Shaking and shaking.

"WHY! THERE you are, naughty Daisy," the farmer said. "You make me hunt for you every day! What can I do about you?"

And he thought and thought. "I have an idea!" the farmer said one day. "I'll soon put a stop to Daisy's game!"

And that night, when Daisy was fast asleep, he hung a big bell around her neck.

Next day he went as usual to bring the cows home, and when he counted them as they came through the gate there were:

1, 2, 3, 4, 5, 6, 7, 8, 9 — but NO DAISY!

Nine good cows but NO DAISY!

But he didn't go to look for her. No. He listened.

And coming from behind a bush, he heard, "Cling clang, cling clang."

It was the bell clanging as Daisy's big, fat body shook and shook with laughter! "Hoo-Hoo! Hoo-Hoo!"

CLING CLANG! CLING CLANG!

And although Daisy wasn't at all pleased at being found so quickly, the farmer was very happy.

Now he could *hear* where she was, because of the bell around her neck!

He would never, never have to hunt again for . . . NAUGHTY DAISY.

Too BIG

Sarah Hayes

There was once a giant who lived in a house on top of a hill. At the bottom of the hill stood a little town. The people in the town were afraid of the giant. They called him "Too Big."

But Too Big was a gentle sort of giant with a very soft heart. And he was lonely. He wanted to be friends with the people from the town. Once he even invited them to dinner.

"We can't possibly go," said the mayor. "He's far too big. His giant's feet would squash us all. And how would we sit down on his enormous chairs? After all, he is the biggest giant in the world."

Then the mayor wrote Too Big a letter saying that everyone was too busy to come to dinner. After that, the giant stayed in his house on the hill and never came out.

Sometimes children came to play on the slopes below the giant's house, and one day a little girl climbed right up to his front door and began to bounce her ball against it. Too Big heard the knocking of the ball and hurried to open the huge door. When they saw the giant, the children screamed and ran away. All except one, and that was the little girl with the ball, whose name was Elspeth. When she saw the giant, Elspeth took a step back.

"Hmm," she said, "you *are* big."

"Yes," said the giant sadly. "Too big."

"Nonsense!" said Elspeth. "Can I come in?"

Then Too Big told Elspeth all about the invitation he had sent. "The mayor said everyone was too busy to come," said the giant.

"Nonsense!" said Elspeth again. "They're just chicken!" Then she had an idea.

A week later an enormous striped tent appeared outside the town. It was the biggest tent in the world. A long line of people waited patiently at the entrance. And inside the tent Elspeth and Too Big the giant began to serve the biggest ice cream cones in the world.

When the mayor saw the biggest ice cream cones in the world, he marched up to the tent.

"Those ice cream cones are too big!" he shouted. "They'll make you sick!"

"Nonsense!" shouted everyone else, and for once the mayor had nothing to say.

All summer long Too Big and Elspeth served ice cream, and the giant was happy. But when winter came, it was too cold for ice cream. The giant had to take down his tent and go home. Biting winds swept through the huge house on the hill. Too Big shivered with cold and misery. None of his friends from the town ever came to visit him now, not even Elspeth.

The fact is that Elspeth was far too busy to visit the giant. And so, for that matter, was everyone else in the town. If Too Big had climbed down the hill and listened at the locks and keyholes, he would have heard a mysterious clicking noise coming from every house in the town, even from the mayor's. CLICK-A-TA, CLICK-A-TA, CLICK-A-TA went the noise. But Too Big didn't climb down the hill, and he didn't hear the mysterious CLICK-A-TA, CLICK-A-TA, CLICK-A-TA noise. He just stayed indoors and felt miserable.

Then, one morning, Too Big heard someone knocking on his front door. No one was there, but on his doorstep lay an enormous package. Slowly the giant undid the wrappings. Slowly he lifted the present out and held it over his head. Then he pushed his arms into the armholes and pulled his present down over his head. Over his chest it went, over his tummy, and right down . . . over . . . his knees. It was the biggest sweater in the world, and it was . . . too big!

"Oh no!" said Elspeth, who had been hiding behind a rock.

"It's too big," said the mayor, who had been hiding too.

"Far too big," said everyone else from a hundred different hiding places.

"Nonsense!" said the giant. "It's perfect!"

And when everyone woke up in the cold of the next morning, they found the biggest trailer in the world parked outside the town. Inside the trailer sat the giant in the biggest sweater in the world. And he was serving out the biggest baked potatoes in the world. And no one, not even the mayor, said the words "too big" ever again.

BECAUSE OF FIGS

Ann Cameron

In the summer I like to lie in the grass and look at clouds and eat figs. Figs are soft and purple and delicious. Their juice runs all over my face, and I eat them till I'm so full I can't eat any more.

Because of figs I got a strange birthday present, and because of that birthday present I had some trouble. This is what happened.

It all started a long time ago when I had my fourth birthday. My father came home from work and said, "I have something for you, Julian! Go and look in the car."

I ran to look, and Huey ran after me, tripping on his shoelaces.

When we looked on the back seat of the car, there was a tree! A small tree with just a few leaves.

We ran back to my father. "A tree for a birthday present!" I said.

"A tree for a birthday present!" Huey said. He was two years old, and he always repeated everything I said.

"It's a fig tree," my father told me. "It will grow as fast as you grow, Julian, and in a few years it will have figs that you can pick and eat."

I could hardly wait to grow my own sweet juicy purple figs. We planted the tree by our back fence, and I gave it water every day. And then one morning it had two new leaves.

"Fig tree, you're growing!" I said. I thought I should be growing

too. There is a mark on the wall in the bathroom of our house, where my father measures us, and I ran into the house to measure myself against my old mark. I pressed my hand against my head, flat to the wall, and checked where my hand was compared to the old mark. I wasn't any taller.

I walked outside to the fig tree. "I'm not any taller," I said. I touched the fig tree's new leaves. "I want to grow, too!" I said. "You know how to grow, and I don't!" I told the fig tree.

The fig tree didn't say a word.

"Maybe what makes you grow will make me grow," I told it. And very quickly I picked the fig tree's new leaves and ate them. They tasted worse than spinach. I was pretty sure they would make me grow.

I did a little growing dance around the fig tree, with my hands raised high in the air.

It worked. I stayed taller than Huey. I got taller than my fig tree. And every time my fig tree got new leaves, I saw them and ate them secretly. And when nobody was looking, I did a growing dance.

"If you don't like this, fig tree, just tell me," I'd say.

The fig tree never said a word.

After a year my father looked at my fig tree. "It's a nice little tree," he said, "but it isn't growing." And he started putting fertilizer on my tree, and he looked at it more often.

But when new leaves showed, I saw them first. And I wanted to get taller, so I ate them.

Another whole year went by.

My mark on the bathroom wall went up three inches. I was four inches taller than Huey, and my arm muscle was twice as big as his.

The fig tree hadn't grown at all.

"Fig tree," I said, when I took its new leaves, "I'm sorry, but I want to grow tall."

And the fig tree didn't say a word.

One day my father was in the garden. He walked over to my fig tree. "Julian," he said, "something is the matter with your tree. It hasn't grown. It hasn't grown at all."

"Really?" I said. I didn't look at my father. I didn't look at my fig tree either.

"Do you have any idea what could be wrong?" my father asked.

I looked straight at my feet. I crossed my toes inside my shoes.

"Oh no."

"I think that tree's just plain no good. We'll pull it out of the ground and get another one."

"Oh no! Don't do that!" I begged.

"Julian," my father said, "do you know something about this tree that I don't know?"

I didn't say anything. And I was glad, very glad, that the fig tree didn't say a word. Finally I said, "It's my tree. Give it one more chance."

"No use waiting around!" my father said. His hand was around the trunk of my tree.

"Please!" I said.

My father's hand relaxed. "After all, it *is* your tree," he said. "Just tell me when you want another one."

All afternoon I couldn't think of anything but all the little fig leaves I'd eaten. I was pretty sure I knew why the fig tree didn't grow.

At bedtime I couldn't sleep, and when Huey went to sleep, I got up and sneaked outside to my fig tree. I told God I knew that the fig leaves belonged to the fig tree. I told the fig tree I was sorry, and I promised I would never eat its leaves again.

The fig tree didn't say a word — but the next week it got two new leaves and kept them. That night I went to bed happy, and I dreamed a good dream. My fig tree was higher than the house, I was almost as tall as my dad, and there were big figs, juicy figs, sweet figs, falling all over the lawn.

THE MAGPIE'S NEST

Michael Rosen

Once a long time ago, when winter was nearly over and spring had nearly begun, all the birds were busy starting to build their nests. There they all were: the robin and the eagle, the seagull, the blackbird, the duck, the owl, and the hummingbird, all busy. All, that is, except Magpie. And she didn't feel much like working.

It was a nice day and she was out and about looking for scrips and scraps and bibs and bobs for her collection of old junk — her hoard of bits and pieces she had picked up from behind chimneys or from drainpipes. Pebbles, beads, buttons, and the like, anything bright and interesting or unusual, Magpie was sure to collect. Just as she was flying along on the lookout for a new treasure, she caught sight of Sparrow, her mouth full of bits of straw and twigs.

"What are you doing, what are you doing?" said Magpie.

"Building my nest," said Sparrow, "like you'll have to soon." "Oh yes?" said Magpie.

"Yes," said Sparrow, "put that milk-bottle top down and come over here and watch. First you have to find a twig, and then another twig, another twig, another twig, another twig . . ."

"Don't make me laugh," said Magpie, "I know, I know, I know all that," and off she flew. And as she flew on, looking for scrips and scraps and bibs and bobs, she came up to Duck, who was upside down with her mouth full of mud.

"What are you doing, what are you doing?" said Magpie.

"Building my nest," said Duck, "like you'll have to soon."

"Oh yes?" said Magpie.

"Yes," said Duck, "throw away that old earwig and watch me. After you've got all your twigs you have to stick them with mud pats like this — pat-pat, pat-pat, pat-pat . . ."

"Don't make me laugh," said Magpie, "I know, I know, I know all that," and off she flew. And as she flew on, looking for scrips and scraps and bibs and bobs, she saw Pigeon with a mouthful of feathers.

"What are you doing, what are you doing?" said Magpie.

"Building my nest," said Pigeon, "like you'll have to soon."

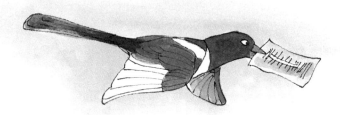

"Oh yes?" said Magpie.

"Yes," said Pigeon, "put that bus ticket down and come over here and learn how. You have to make yourself warm and cozy — right? Right. So you dig your beak into your chest like this — right? And find one of those very soft fluffy feathers down there and you lay that out very carefully inside your nest to keep it warm and cozy, warm and cozy, warm and cozy . . ."

"Don't make me laugh," said Magpie, "I know, I know, I know, I know all that," and off she flew.

Well, not long after that it was time for Magpie to lay her eggs, and she looked out from her perch and saw all the other birds sitting in their well-built, warm, cozy nests, laying their eggs. "Oh no," said Magpie, "I haven't got anywhere to lay mine! I'd better hurry." And she remembered Sparrow saying something about twigs, and Duck about patting them, and Pigeon saying something about cozy feathers. So she rushed out and quickly grabbed as many twigs as she could, made a great pile of them, threw a feather on the top — and the milk-bottle top and the earwig and the bus ticket, and she *just* had time to sit herself down and lay her eggs.

And if you look at a magpie's nest you'll see it's always a mess. And she ends up throwing her scrips and scraps and bibs and bobs in it too.

I think she likes it like that.

SUNDAY BOOTS AND WORKING BOOTS

Annette Penny

In a closet under the stairs of a little cottage lived two pairs of boots. Their names were Sunday Boots and Working Boots. They belonged to a man called Dad.

"Missus," he said to his wife on Sunday mornings, "have you seen my Sunday boots?"

"Yes, Dad," Missus answered. "They're under the stairs all cleaned and polished, ready to wear to church."

On hearing this, Sunday Boots gleamed wickedly in the dim light of the closet.

"See, you dirty old working boots," they said. "We are off to church. Only the best boots are worn to church. You will never be worn to church. You are much too old and dirty!"

Sunday Boots, although smart and shiny, were not nice at all. In fact they were very nasty, particularly to Working Boots.

Dad was a farmer, and he wore Working Boots while he worked in the fields from Mondays to Saturdays. The fields were muddy, and the mud stuck to Working Boots. This happened so often that Dad said to Missus, "It's not worth cleaning my old working boots because they will only get covered with mud again tomorrow."

So Working Boots got dirtier and dirtier, muddier and muddier, and Sunday Boots hissed, "Get away from us, you filthy boots! We don't want you spoiling our shiny black polish! We can't understand why Dad puts you in the closet with us."

"We're sorry," said Working Boots sadly, "but we can't help being muddy."

Sunday Boots stuck their tongues out at Working Boots and said rudely, "Be quiet. We are going to sing.

We are going to sing one of the beautiful songs we hear when we are in church."

And they sang "All Things Bright and Beautiful."

"That was lovely, Sunday Boots," said Working Boots. "You do sing well."

"Of course," Sunday Boots said grandly. "But then we are of the very best leather. We doubt dirty things like you can sing, even if you know any songs."

"Oh, we know one song," said Working Boots eagerly. "Dad sings it when we are out in the fields. It goes like this."

They began to sing sweetly "My Old Man's a Garbageman."

"Stop! Stop!" shrieked Sunday Boots. "What a dreadfully common song, and what dreadfully common voices!"

They turned on their heels and settled themselves in the corner of the closet as far away from Working Boots as they could get.

One day, as Dad was pulling on Working Boots, ready

for work, Missus said, "Dad, those old boots of yours are quite worn out. You'll have to buy some more."

Dad nodded his head. "Yes, you're right, Missus. There are two big holes in them that are quite past mending."

Working Boots were horrified.

"What ever is going to happen to us?" they whispered fearfully to Sunday Boots when they were put away for the night.

"Why, don't you know?" sneered Sunday Boots. "You won't be needed anymore. You'll be thrown away and you'll be able to sing "My Old Man's a Garbageman" all the way to the dump where they put all the rest of the trash."

Working Boots felt sad and frightened. They did not feel any happier when, next day, Dad took Sunday Boots out of the closet and, although it was not yet Sunday, put them on to wear to the store. All day long Working Boots stood by themselves in the closet.

"Oh dear," they sighed, "we really don't want to be thrown onto the trash dump. We like it here, even if Sunday Boots are horrible to us."

Great tears fell from their lace holes.

When Dad and Missus came home, Dad placed a brand-new pair of boots in the closet. He picked up Working Boots and took

them into the backyard. He was just about to throw them into the trash can when he said, "You know, Missus, these old boots have been very good to me all these years. It seems a shame to throw them away." Suddenly he smiled and said, "I don't think I will throw them away. I've an idea."

Dad carried Working Boots to the shed and closed the door behind him.

Some time later, Dad came into the kitchen and beamed at Missus. He held out Working Boots. They were no longer dirty, but sparkling clean. Dad had brushed them thoroughly and given them a good coat of varnish. And in them he had planted two beautiful geraniums.

"My, my," Missus said in delight, "those boots make lovely planters. They will look just right on my kitchen windowsill."

Working Boots were overjoyed. From that day onward they sat on the sill proudly holding their geraniums.

And what did Dad wear now when he went out to work in the fields?

Well, of course he did not want to spoil his smart new boots. So he wore Sunday Boots for work from Monday to Saturday. And soon they became muddy. Very muddy indeed.

THE LITTLE ELEPHANT'S NEXT BEST THING

Mary Rayner

There was once a little elephant who lived in the hills of South India, with his mother and all his aunties in the teak forest.

One day he was splashing about in the river while his mother was being bathed. He squirted water at the other young elephants, and they squealed and squirted back. Then the little elephant looked up and saw a balloon floating high in the sky. And underneath the balloon was a basket, and in the basket, just looking at the view, was a man. "I would like to do that," thought the little elephant. "It would be better than splashing, better than squirting. It would be the next best thing to flying."

He asked his mother how he could go up in a balloon.

"Don't be silly," said his mother. "You are too small."

So the little elephant waited for the weeks to go by, and then he asked one of the aunties.

"Don't be silly," said the aunty. "You are too heavy."

"Oh dear," thought the little elephant. "First I was too small and now I'm too heavy. I will eat less, and *then* I will be able to go up in a balloon."

So he stopped crunching up bamboo leaves, and every time he was hungry he thought about floating through the sky, until the man who looked after the elephants said:

"Dear me, this little elephant is getting too thin. Little elephant, what is the matter?"

The little elephant said, "I want to be thin because then I will not be too heavy to go up in a balloon."

"Ay yai," said the man. "But little elephant, you are *growing*, you will soon be too big."

The little elephant began to cry.

"It is not too late," said the man kindly. "We will get a balloon made. Soon, soon. All we need is money." So he thought and he thought, and then he said, "Little elephant, come with me, and we shall go to the town."

They waved good-bye to the little elephant's mother and all the aunties, and set off together for the big town. They walked along the hot, dusty road for miles and, miles, past fields of sugarcane and groves of coconut palms and across a dry riverbed.

"I am thirsty," said the little elephant.

"Soon, soon, we will be there," said the man.

They came to a stand beside the road, next to a garage. The elephant man asked for a cup of tea, and a drink for his elephant. The elephant filled his trunk with water from a bucket, squirted the water into his mouth and drank it all down. The man got some more.

Just then a bus drew up, full of people. The driver got out and said, "I need gas, and no one can see out of the windows because they are so dusty."

The little elephant became very excited. "I will squirt the windows clean," he said.

"Tell all your passengers to give money," said the elephant man, "and my elephant will clean your bus."

So the little elephant squirted water all over the bus, and all the passengers were pleased and gave tips to the elephant man.

When the bus had gone, the garage man said, "That

was good. If you would like to stay in the field behind my stand and garage, you can clean all the buses that stop here. Everyone likes your elephant."

So the elephant man and the little elephant stayed for many weeks, until they had cleaned a great many buses and saved up a great deal of money.

"Now it is time to go to the town," said the elephant man. They waved good-bye to the garage man and set off again along the hot, dusty road to the town. They went to find the man who made hot-air balloons.

The elephant man explained that the little elephant wanted to ride in a balloon.

The balloon maker shook his head. "That is not possible," he said. "Your elephant is too heavy."

"Can't you make me one specially?" asked the elephant man.

"Not possible," said the balloon maker.

"We can pay," said the elephant man, and he tipped out fat bundles of rupees in a heap on the ground.

"Perhaps possible after all," said the balloon maker. "Come back in three weeks."

The little elephant and his friend went away, and they waited for three weeks, and then they came back again.

The balloon maker had made a beautiful orange-and-yellow balloon. It lay on the ground behind his shop, and tied onto it was an enormous basket, an elephant-sized basket with some extra space for the elephant man.

"Now I will tell you how to do it," said the balloon maker, and he showed them how to fill the balloon with hot air to make it rise up into the sky.

So the balloon was filled with hot air, and just as it lifted off the ground, the little elephant and his friend scrambled into the basket. Up into the sky they went, and they waved good-bye to the balloon maker. Slowly all the white houses of the town and even the big palace became tiny, tinier than toys. They floated along above the dusty road, over the dry riverbed and over the coconut palms and over the sugarcane fields until they came toward the hills.

On their way they saw the garage and the stand, and they waved, and the garage man waved back and cheered and clapped. And they passed a bus full of tourists, and they waved, and the bus driver and all the tourists waved back and cheered and clapped.

It was just getting to be evening when at last they came to the teak forest. Now they could see the river. They came down a little lower, and the little elephant began to squeal and trumpet, because he could see his mother and all the aunties being bathed.

All the big old elephants looked up, and they saw the great orange-and-yellow balloon, and the little elephant waving his trunk, and his friend beside him.

"Just look at my son!" said his mother, and she put up her trunk and trumpeted to him.

The balloon came down on the ground, and the little elephant climbed out. His mother and all the aunties welcomed him back, and all the young elephants had an extra splashy and squirty game with him because he had been away for so long.

IT'S A GOOD HONEST NAME

Dick King-Smith

Mr. and Mrs. Doddipoll's first baby was a boy. He was a very long baby.

"What shall we call him?" said Mr. Doddipoll.

"John," said Mrs. Doddipoll. "It's a good honest name."

A year later Mrs. Doddipoll had a second baby. It was another boy.

"What shall we call him?" said Mr. Doddipoll.

"John," said Mrs. Doddipoll. "It's a good honest name."

The father looked a bit worried. "We've got one John," he said.

"We can easily tell them apart," said the mother. "This one's not going to be tall like his brother. He's going to be short."

So they called the new baby Short John and his elder brother Long John.

Another year passed, and another baby was born, a little brother for Long John and Short John.

"Another John, I suppose?" said Mr. Doddipoll.

"Naturally," said Mrs. Doddipoll. This baby was a skinny little chap, so of course he was called Thin John.

And guess what — after another year along came a fourth brother, who was very tubby. By now the father had given up asking silly questions about what to call a new baby. He just took one look at the child and said, "Fat John?"

"Of course," said the mother. "Bring the others to see him."

Thin John, who was one year old, took a look and said, "Wah!"

Short John, who was two, said, "Bay-bee!"

And Long John, who was three and already very tall, said, "John!"

"Fat John," said his parents.

"Look!" said Long John to Short John and Thin John, pointing into the cradle. "Look! Fat John!"

"Bay-bee!" said Short John.

"Wah!" said Thin John.

One day when the four Johns were another year older, they went for a walk together. Short John (who was strong) gave Thin John (who was light) a piggyback ride. This made them together as tall as Long John (who was carrying Fat John in his arms). It was a lovely day.

When they finally got back home again, their father was standing in the doorway looking out for them.

"Hello, Johns," said Mr. Doddipoll. "I've got a surprise for you. Guess what?"

Long John put Fat John down on the ground.

"Mother's had another baby?" he said.

Short John lifted Thin John off his shoulders.

"'Nother John?" he said.

"Bay-bee," said Thin John.

"Wah!" said Fat John.

"Yes, there's another baby," said Mr. Doddipoll. "But we're not going to call this one John."

"You're not going to call it John, Father?" said Long John in an unhappy voice. "It's a good honest name."

The other three boys looked miserable.

"No more Johns?" said Short John sadly.

"Poor b-bay-bee!" moaned Thin John.

And as for Fat John, he burst into floods of tears.

"Wah! Wah! Wah!" he yelled.

Mr. Doddipoll put his arms around the four Johns, and when Fat John had stopped yelling he said, "There's a good reason, you see, why we're not going to call this one John. Because it's a girl. Come and see her."

"Hello, Johns," said Mrs. Doddipoll. "What do you think of your new baby sister?"

The four Johns looked at the baby girl, but they did not answer, except for Fat John, who said, "Wah!" very softly, under his breath.

"We're going to call her Janet," said Mrs. Doddipoll.

But the funny thing is that the four John Doddipolls never did call her by her real name. They grew up to be men, and they lived to be old men, and they looked after their only sister well.

But neither Long John, nor Short John, nor Thin John, nor Fat John ever called her Janet.

They called her Girl John. After all, it's a good honest name.

THE CLETTERKIN

Jenny Koralek

One morning after breakfast, Leggie Meggie ran into the garden to play with her new, yellow, very small, bouncy ball. And after one bounce she lost it. She rushed indoors, calling, "Mom! Dad! Grannie! I've lost my new best ball!"

"I can't help you now," said Dad crossly. "I've lost my car keys. I will have to walk to work and I'll be very late."

"What we need in this house," said Grannie, "is a cletterkin."

But Dad didn't hear. He had gone, banging the door behind him.

"And I can't help you," said Mom. "I've lost my glasses. I've hunted high and low. I won't be able to read my book on the way to work and I'll be late too."

"What we need in this house," said Grannie, "is a cletterkin."

But Mom didn't hear. She had gone, banging the door behind her.

Leggie Meggie heard.

"What's a cletterkin?" she said.

Grannie looked up from her knitting. "A cletterkin finds things," she said. "And tidies what's untidy. A

cletterkin can see into all the little nooks and crannies, indoors and out, where balls roll and car keys fall and glasses lie. When I was a girl every house had a cletterkin."

"What does a cletterkin look like?" asked Leggie Meggie.

"I've never seen one myself," said Grannie. She stopped to pick up a stitch from her knitting. "But . . ."

"But what?" said Leggie Meggie.

"Once I met a man who'd met a man who said . . . a cletterkin has furry feet and leafy hair. He moves on feet as soft as cats' paws. He can shoot up as tall as a tree and shrink as small as a mouse. And because he can hunt high and low, he can find high and low. I never saw the cletterkin in our house, but I know, I just know he was the one who always found my lost pocket-money penny and my brother's best blue marble."

"What was that noise?" said Leggie Meggie.

"What noise?" said Grannie.

"Soft on the floorboards like cats' paws," said Leggie Meggie.

"I heard nothing," yawned Grannie. "And now, oh dear, I've lost my knitting needle. I tell you, what we need in this house is a cletterkin."

She yawned again and began to nod off in her chair.

Leggie Meggie went back into the garden to look for her ball. She looked in the long grass. She looked under

the bushes. She got a stick and poked in the stinging nettles. Where could it be?

"Perhaps it fell into one of the flowerpots," she said. She looked in three flowerpots. They were empty, except one that had a little bed of dry leaves and some snail shells full of raindrops. She was just about to put her hand into another flowerpot when a voice said:

"Didn't you know, long-leggedy, it's very rude to

scrabble about in people's houses? You've just unmade my bed and tipped over my cups."

There, by the flowerpot with the bed of dry leaves and the snail shells full of raindrops, was a little man with leafy hair and furry feet. He was sitting on Leggie Meggie's new, yellow, very small, bouncy ball.

"A cletterkin!" cried Leggie Meggie. "Just like Grannie said!"

"Not *a* cletterkin," said the little man. "*The* cletterkin, the *last* cletterkin."

"What happened to the others?" asked Leggie Meggie.

"They went away long ago to look for the rainbow's end," said the cletterkin.

"Oh dear," said Leggie Meggie.

"They'll never find it."

"I know," sighed the cletterkin.

"Don't be sad," said Leggie Meggie. "We need you in our house. Grannie says so every day because we're always losing things. Just in one morning I've lost my ball, Dad's lost his car keys, Mom's lost her glasses, and Grannie's lost her knitting needle! Oh, won't you be our cletterkin?"

"Well," said the cletterkin briskly, "you do sound like a very untidy family!" But he made that sound like something good. "If you've lost all those things since you got up this morning, who knows what you'll have lost by bedtime. I'd better get started right away."

So Leggie Meggie led the way into the house. She showed the cletterkin the cat flap.

"You can always come in and out through there," she whispered, "when I'm not here to let you in. Because we will keep you a secret, won't we?"

"Of course," said the cletterkin, "and anyway I have a little trick. I can make myself invisible if I want to."

"Go on then," said Leggie Meggie.

Suddenly the cletterkin had vanished, but Leggie Meggie heard his voice singing, "Cletter cletter, that's better." Then something scuttled through the newspaper lying like a tent on the floor, and there were Mom's glasses lying at Grannie's feet.

"Cletter cletter, that's better," came a voice from somewhere near the front door. "Car keys in an old shoe! There's enough work here for a hundred years."

There was a scurrying of feet as soft as cats' paws, and there were Dad's keys lying at Grannie's feet.

"Cletter cletter, that's better," sang the invisible cletterkin, and Grannie's knitting needle seemed to heave itself up from a wide crack in the floorboards.

And there he was, sitting on top of Grannie's wool basket.

Just then the door banged and Leggie Mcggie heard her mother calling.

"I must go now," she said.

"And I'm off to my house," said the cletterkin.

"I'll come out and play later," whispered Leggie Meggie, and the cletterkin shot out through the cat flap.

When Mom and Dad saw all the lost things laid out at Grannie's feet, they were very pleased.

"Good girl, Leggie Meggie," said Dad.

"It wasn't me," said Leggie Meggie.

"Was it Grannie then?" They smiled at Grannie sleeping in her chair. "Dear Grannie, no wonder she's tired."

Then Grannie woke up. She saw her lost knitting needle neatly stuck into her wool. She saw Leggie Meggie holding her new, yellow, very small, bouncy ball. She saw the keys and Mom's glasses lying by her feet.

"Well," she said. "Perhaps there is a cletterkin here, after all."

THE LITTLE BOY'S SECRET

David L. Harrison

One day a little boy left school early because he had a secret to tell his mother. He was in a hurry to get home, so he took a shortcut through some woods where three terrible giants lived. He hadn't gone far before he met one of them standing in the path.

When the giant saw the little boy, he put his hands on his hips and roared, "What are you doing here, boy? Don't you know whose woods these are?"

"I'm on my way home," answered the little boy. "I have a secret to tell my mother."

That made the giant furious. "Secret?" he bellowed. "What secret?"

"I can't tell you," said the little

boy, "or it wouldn't be a secret anymore."

"Then I'm taking you to our castle!" said the giant. Stooping down, he picked up the little boy and popped him into his shirt pocket.

Before long the first giant met a second giant, who was twice as big, three times as ugly, and four times as fierce. "What's that in your pocket?" he asked the first giant.

"A boy," he answered. "Says he has a secret that he won't tell us."

When the second giant heard that, he laughed a wicked laugh. "Won't tell us, eh?" he chuckled. "Well, we'll just see about that! To the castle with him!"

The giants thumped on down the path. In a short time they came to a huge stone castle beside a muddy river.

At the door they met the third giant, who was five times bigger, six times uglier, and seven times fiercer than the second giant.

"What's that in your pocket?" he asked the first giant.

"A boy," he answered.

"A boy!" chuckled the third giant. He brought his huge eye close to the pocket and peered in.

"Says he has a secret he won't tell us," said the first giant.

When the third giant heard that, he laughed a terrible laugh. "Won't tell us, eh?" he asked. "Well, we'll just see about that! On the table with him!"

The first giant took the little boy from his pocket and set him on the kitchen table. Then all three giants gathered around and peered down at him.

The little boy looked at the first giant. He looked at the second giant. He looked at the third giant.

They were truly enormous and dreadful to behold.

"Well?" said the first giant.

"We're waiting," said the second giant.

"I'll count to three," said the third giant. "One...two..."

The little boy sighed a big sigh.

"Oh, all right," he said. "I suppose I can tell you. But if I do, you must promise to let me go."

"We promise," answered the giants. But they all winked sly winks at one another and crossed their fingers behind their backs because they didn't really mean to let him go at all.

The little boy turned to the first giant. "Bend down," he said. The giant leaned down and the little boy whispered into his ear.

When the giant heard the secret, he leaped up from the table. His knees shook. His tongue hung out. "Oh no!" he shouted. "That's terrible!" And he dashed from the castle, ran deep into the woods, and climbed to the top of a tall tree. He didn't come down for three days.

The second giant scowled at the little boy.

"What's wrong with him?" he asked.

"Never mind," said the little boy. "Just bend down."

The giant leaned down, and the little boy stood on tiptoe and whispered into his ear.

When the giant heard the secret, he leaped up so fast that he knocked his chair over. His eyes rolled. His ears twitched. "Let me get away!" he roared. And he raced from the castle, ran over the hills, and crawled into the deepest, darkest cave he could find.

The third giant frowned down at the little boy.

"What's wrong with them?" he asked.

"Never mind," said the little boy. "Just bend down."

The giant leaned down and the little boy climbed onto a teacup and whispered into his ear.

When the giant heard the secret, he jumped up so fast that he ripped the seat of his trousers. His teeth chattered. His hair stood on end. "Help!" he cried. "Help!" And he dashed from the castle and dove headfirst into the muddy river.

The castle door had been left open, and since the giants had promised the little boy that he could go, he walked out and went home.

At last he was able to tell his mother his secret, but she didn't yell and run away. She just put him to bed and gave him some supper.

The next morning when the little boy woke up, he was covered from head to toe with bright red spots.

"Now I can tell *everybody* what my secret was," he said with a smile. "My secret was . . . . I'M GETTING THE MEASLES!"

SALLY'S WOOLLY ELEPHANT

Adèle Geras

Sally's woolly elephant, dressed in his striped woolly scarf, thought it was a lovely afternoon for a walk.

All the tree trunks and branches were frosty and glittering in the sun, the roofs were white and shining, the leaves and grass were sprinkled with icy powder.

"How pretty it looks," thought Sally's woolly elephant, "and how pleasant it is to feel warm. It's good to be a woolly elephant on a cold afternoon."

At that moment he saw a robin sitting on a gate.

"Hello, robin," he said. "Splendid day, isn't it?"

"I suppose it looks splendid," agreed the robin, "but it's chilly all the same. Could I ride on your back as far as the park? My feet are very cold."

"I'm afraid I can't let you do that," said Sally's woolly elephant. "Your feet are dirty and I don't want mud on my woolly back. Hope you don't mind. Good-bye."

And the woolly elephant shuffled off through the crisp leaves.

"Hello, woolly elephant," cried the pigeons outside the library. "Chilly, isn't it? Could we ride on your warm back as far as the bakery? The baker throws out a lot of crumbs on Tuesdays, and it's a long way in this weather."

"I'd like to take you," said the woolly elephant, "but there are a lot of you and you'd make my back very dirty, so I must say no, I'm afraid. Bye-bye."

And away he slid on the frozen puddles.

"Hello, woolly elephant," said the small kitten who was sitting on the step outside the butcher shop. "You look warm and cozy. I like your stripey scarf. Would you lend it to me while I wait here? I'll have to wait a long time before I get any scraps, you know, and walking will keep you warm."

"I'm sorry, kitten," said Sally's woolly elephant, "but it's my very own *special* scarf, and I wouldn't like to part with it. Good-bye."

And he slipped along the slippery sidewalk.

At last the woolly elephant reached the park. He walked down the gray paths, looked at the frozen pink roses left over from the summer, smiled at the babies bundled into their warm baby carriages, waved his trunk at the old men in black hats sitting on the benches, and made his way to the swings.

"Isn't it cold, woolly elephant?" shouted the children as he swung himself through the air.

"Not if you're a woolly elephant," he replied, and he sang this little song as the swing went up and down:

"When the weather's cold and icy
  Being woolly's very nicey;
  Being chilly's very silly
  But it's bully to be woolly!"

Sally's elephant was having such fun that he forgot the time. The sun went down, the lamps were already glowing in the street outside the park.

"Gosh, it's late," said the woolly elephant. "I must go home or Sally will be worried."

Just then the mist came down, muffling the trees, hiding the houses, blanketing the lights. The woolly elephant could see the tip of his trunk and that was all.

"How will I ever get home?" he thought. "I can't see the way. I'll miss my supper. I'll have to stay out all night with no one to talk to. Whatever will I do?"

And he began to cry.

"Don't cry, woolly elephant," said a small voice down near his feet. "It's me, the kitten from the butcher shop. I'll help you to find your way home. I was chasing a bird, and the mist came down just before I caught it."

The kitten jumped onto the woolly elephant's back and guided him to the street. Cats can see in the dark. When they came to the butcher shop, the kitten jumped off.

"There you are, woolly elephant. Just follow the street-lights and you'll soon be home."

"Thank you," said the woolly elephant. "I'm sorry I didn't lend you my scarf. You may borrow it now if you're cold."

"You keep it for the moment," said the kitten, "but I'd love to wear it for a while tomorrow."

"You'll have it for as long as you like," said Sally's woolly elephant, and he plodded away into the mist.

"It must be awfully late," he thought. "There's no one around. I think I'm a bit frightened, and I know I'm lonely."

Suddenly he heard a rush of wings, and a whole flock of pigeons settled on his back. "Don't be frightened," they cooed. "We'll sing to you and cheer you up."

They sat on the elephant's back, singing happy songs into his woolly ears until he came to the traffic lights.

"I'll take you for a ride again tomorrow," he told them as they flew off. "I'm sorry I didn't take you when you

asked. I hope you had lots of crumbs to eat. Good night."

Sally's woolly elephant was nearly home now, but the mist was so thick that he could not read the street signs.

"Oh dear," he sighed. "Is it this one or the next one? I'll never find it. What shall I do?"

"Come with me," said the robin, settling on the elephant's trunk. "I'll show you the street and the house."

He flew along just in front of the woolly elephant, and led him right to the back door of Sally's house. Yellow light was pouring out of the kitchen window, and Sally was eating hot buttered toast at the table.

"Thank you so much, robin," said the elephant. "I'm sorry I didn't take you to the park today. Shall we go there together tomorrow?"

"That would be delightful," said the robin. "Good-bye, woolly elephant."

And he disappeared into the branches of the pear tree in the yard next door.

The following day Sally's woolly elephant took the robin on his back and set off for the park. When they reached the library, all the pigeons fluttered down, singing and jostling one another. Just outside the bakery they rose in a gray cloud from the elephant's back, and swooped down to eat the crumbs. At the butcher shop the woolly elephant stopped to lend the kitten his scarf.

When they reached the park, the robin and the woolly elephant had a wonderful time on the swings. And they went home early together, while it was still light.

THE SMALL BOY AND THE LONELY PLACE

John Maguire

One day, in quite a big room in quite a big house, the different places were talking. They were all saying how important and special they were.

"Oh dear, I'm so tired!" said the Place Just Inside The Door. "Everyone walks on me when they come into the room. Then they walk on me again when they go out. I sometimes feel quite exhausted. Still, that's only to be expected —

I'm *quite* the most important place of all."

"Oh yeah, says who?" said the Place In Front Of The Fire. "They mostly come to me. I have the big couch and the armchairs. In the winter I have a lovely hot fire to keep them warm. In the summer I have a beautiful bowl of flowers for

70

them to admire. *I* am where they spend most of their time, all through the year."

Then the Place In Front Of The Window said:

"What about me? I don't need any old flowers. In the summer you can see the whole garden through my big window. Even in the winter you can see all the world outside. Sometimes people stand here, just looking out, for ages. *I* am beautiful *and* important."

"But where would anyone be without me?" asked the Place Under The Shelves. "If anybody wants to put on the stereo, or get down a book, or talk on the telephone, they have to come to me. I must be the most useful place in the room."

Then they all stopped, because they heard a very quiet sound. It was one you would hardly notice.

"Excuse me," said the little dark Place Behind The Armchair. "I just wish I was important or beautiful or useful or something. I think you're *all* very lucky."

"How *dare* you even talk to us!" said the Place Just Inside The Door. "What are you, anyway, only a silly dark corner behind the armchair? Nobody ever goes into or out of you!"

"Yes, indeed," said the Place In Front Of The Fire. "Nobody ever sits down in you to have a nice time. They probably don't even know you're there!"

"Nobody ever sees anything nice or interesting from you!" said the Place In Front Of The Window. "You really aren't an important place at all."

"Look, you haven't even got a carpet!" said the Place Under The Shelves. "All you do is gather dust."

The little dark Place Behind The Armchair didn't say anything more. It was very lonely and wished that it had *something* to feel important or beautiful or useful about. It just wasn't fair.

The next day was *awful*. It was cold and rainy. The clouds were very low, and everywhere was gloomy. All the places in the room were dark and dreary, and nothing nice was happening.

Outside the room there were angry voices in the hall. Mom and Dad and all the children were cranky. Nobody knew what they wanted to do, and nobody wanted to do what anyone else wanted either.

Then the door of the room opened quite quietly. A

small boy came in. He was the youngest of the family, and he was having a terrible day. Everyone was cross; everyone was fed up; everyone said "No!" even before he was able to ask them anything. Nobody wanted to play with him, and he kept getting in everybody's way.

So the small boy had come into the room. He wanted some quiet time on his own. He knew the way that awful days like this went. His parents had told him to go away, but in a few minutes they would be looking for him crossly. They'd want him to tidy his room or put away his pencils or help with the dishes or something. He was going to keep out of their way and have a good quiet time all to himself.

He stood just inside the door for a minute. Then he went over and stood by the shelves. Then he stood in front of the fireplace. Then he went over and looked out of the window. But he didn't feel better in any of these places. He looked around, and suddenly he noticed something new — there was a very secret, dark little cornery place behind the big armchair.

He went right over and wriggled in there. It was a small place, but then he was a small boy and that suited him very well. It was a very quiet place, but that was just right because he wanted a very quiet time.

"I think this is a *great* new place," said the boy out loud. "It's just what I wanted. It's nice and small and quiet, and nobody has to come here to do things, so I can hide here whenever I want to. It hasn't even got a carpet, so if I drop cracker crumbs or spill lemonade, I can wipe it up and no one will ever know.

"This place is going to be my special hideaway. It'll be my secret cubbyhole. It's just great."

All the other places could hear the small boy talking, and for once they were at a loss for words. The small boy and the lonely place were going to get on fine.

THE BIRTHDAY GIFT

Sally Grindley

On the corner of a narrow street lost on the edge of town stood a little junk shop. Its long-unwashed windows were all flaky paint and cobwebs, and you could barely see in. If you pressed your nose hard against the glass, you could see shelves crammed with a higgledy-piggledy assortment of pots and pans and vases and candlesticks and books and pictures and oh so many things that you didn't know where to look. Most of them were dust gatherers and had been there forever. But hanging in the corner was a beautiful string puppet of a clown. One of its strings was broken, but otherwise it was just like new, and its smile beamed out through the dirt all around.

Amy and her father often passed the shop but never bothered to look in. Then one day Amy stopped and pressed her nose up against the filthy window. When she

saw the puppet, she jumped up and down excitedly and
called her father over.

"Look at the clown," she said. "Oh, Dad, can I have
him? Please can I have him?"

"We'll see," said her father. "It's your birthday soon."

Amy wanted and wanted and wanted the clown. Every
time they walked near the shop, she rushed up to the
window to make sure he was still there.

"How long is it till my birthday?" she asked her father.

"Four weeks," said her father.

"Is that long?" she said.

"Not long," he replied.

Two weeks later, she asked the same question.

"How long is it till my birthday now?"

"Two weeks," said her father.

"Is that long?" she asked.

"Not long," he replied.

Some days later she asked again.

"Tomorrow," said her father. "It's your birthday tomorrow. We'll go out together to buy your present."

"The clown?" begged Amy.

"If that's what you'd like," said her father.

Amy could hardly sleep that night, she was so excited. And she was restless all morning, until at last her father said that the stores would be open and he was ready to go. She skipped along beside him, chattering away about the clown and how pleased the clown would be to leave the filthy window, and how she would make him dance, and how she would hang him by her bed at night, and how the string needed mending and he would do it, Daddy, wouldn't he? and how her friends would all want to play with him.

At last they reached the junk shop. When they opened the cracked wooden door, a bell rang and an old man hardly taller than Amy appeared behind the counter.

"Can I help you, sir?" he asked.

"Yes," said Amy's father. "I'd like to buy the clown puppet you have hanging in the window. It's my daughter's birthday and she's set her heart on it."

"Many happy returns to you, my dear," said the man. "I'll just go and get him. He's a beautiful piece of work, the best in my shop."

While the man was busy taking the puppet out of the window, a woman came into the shop. She stood by the counter and waited impatiently to be served. The man reappeared and went behind the counter with Amy's clown. He laid it down while he searched for some wrapping paper. When the woman saw the puppet, she let out a cry.

"Wait," she said, "you're not selling that, are you?"

"Why, yes, madam," said the man. "This gentleman is buying it for his daughter's birthday."

"But he can't!" cried the woman. "I must have it. Billy's set his heart on it."

"I'm sorry, madam, but this gentleman was here first."

"I know," said the woman, in despair. "It's just that my son is very ill in the hospital and I promised him the puppet for his birthday. His birthday's not for another four weeks, but I thought if I bought the puppet now it would cheer him up. He's been going on about it for ages."

The man stood in silence and looked at Amy's father. Amy's father looked at Amy. Amy looked down at her clown. With a big effort she said very quietly:

"He can have the clown."

The woman rushed over to her and thanked her over and over again.

"You're a good girl," she said, with tears in her eyes. "I'll tell my Billy what you did for him."

Amy's father picked her up and hugged her.

"We hope Billy gets well soon," he said to the woman.

Amy chose a pair of roller skates instead for her birthday, and it was not too long before she forgot her disappointment over the puppet clown. Then, a few weeks later, she was shopping in town with her father when they saw the woman again. She waved excitedly and ran over to them.

"You're the little girl who gave up the puppet clown for my Billy. I'm glad I bumped into you. Billy's better. He was in the hospital for six weeks, but now he's better. And he loves that clown. He takes it with him everywhere, makes it dance, even hangs it up by his bed at night. Would you like to come over one day and meet Billy?''

Later that week Amy went to see Billy. He showed her the puppet clown, still smiling and with the string mended. Then his mother gave her a box wrapped in "thank you" paper. Amy opened it very carefully, lifted up the cross of wood, disentangled the strings and pulled gently, and out of the box danced — a puppet lion! A shaggy-headed, swishy-tailed, loppy-legged lion with a great big smile. Amy shrieked with joy.

"He's beautiful," she said. "He's so beautiful."

Billy danced his clown over to Amy's lion and they performed the first of many wild and happy jigs together.